HAUNTED CHEMISTRY

LINDSEY R. LOUCKS

Previously released on Entangled's Ever After imprint — September 2013

Entangled Publishing, LLC
2614 South Timberline Road
Suite 109
Fort Collins, CO 80525
Visit our website at www.entangledpublishing.com.

Embrace is an imprint of Entangled Publishing, LLC.

Edited by Kaleen Harding and Libby Murphy
Cover design by Louisa Maggio
Cover art from iStock

Manufactured in the United States of America

First Edition September 2013

embrace

For Jesse, who wants to be a ghost-sniffing cat, but there are just too many naps to take.

Chapter One

Laundry can sure be terrifying when you haven't done it in weeks. I heave the stuffed red bag over my shoulder, Santa-style. The poufy drawstrings smack me in the ear.

"I'll be right back, Tri," I call over my shoulder.

The cat bounds down the hallway toward me as though I've just announced we're out of his favorite salmon treats. I swear he thinks he's part dog. I give him a quick chin rub and he wrinkles his triangle nose, stretching his neck up as far as it'll go. He squints olive-green eyes at me over his white Hitler mustache. It's beyond cute on Tri, not so much on Hitler. He swipes at my ankles with an orange-and-white-striped paw as I open the door.

"We'll play when I get back." I shoo him into the apartment with the side of my sandal. "Watch your twinkle-toes."

I haven't done laundry in this building since I moved in three weeks ago. The landlord said the facilities were downstairs—two washers, two dryers. Hopefully they do more than just eat quarters. My first year in college, I learned how sacred quarters are. No one teaches that in high school, but it's a life lesson every college student needs to know. These words should be stamped on diplomas: *Remember This Always: Quarters Are Sacred.*

Gray clouds chase over the darkening sky. A strong wind brushes past my bare arms. The evening is strangely cool for August in Kansas. It can't rain yet, not until I'm done with my laundry, because I already dried my hair. But if it does rain, maybe it'll be quick. I shiver and start down the stairs. The iron crisscrosses hum under my sandals, sending vibrations through my toes in a steady rhythm.

At the bottom, a red hand-painted sign on a door reads LAUNDRY. Some of the paint from the sign and the door has crumbled to the ground like pulled snake scales. Three of the six squares of dirty glass at the top of the door are broken. No light spills through from inside.

Thunder growls in the distance. The thought of going down there alone pebbles my skin with goose bumps. I could go to the Laundromat later. I could just buy new underwear and socks and call it good for another week or two. But I'm already here, and a spooky dark basement never hurt anyone. Well, it never hurt me, anyway.

As I take a step forward, the door bursts open. My heart leaps into my throat. I cry out. My cheeks heat at the surprised face of Ian Reese, my chemistry lab partner from last year. His hair has been shaved into a buzz cut, accentuating his sharp cheekbones and those blue eyes that shoot static to where my heart should be. A black T-shirt hugs every dip and curve of his muscles, and his jeans hang from his hips in a sexy peel-me-off kind of way.

Holy. Cow.

"Alexis," he says with a smile that could melt the sun. "How are you?"

"Ian." I look away to mentally fan myself. "I'm good. You live here?"

"As of yesterday. I got here late last night." He juts his chin to his right. "Apartment twelve."

"Twenty-six."

He nods. We stand in awkward silence because I can't think of anything else to say. Our date that never happened mixes with the cool air and hangs heavy with the clouds.

"So, two more years, then we're done, huh?" he says.

"Then physical therapy school, but yeah."

"Oh, right." He rolls his lips together. "Chances are we probably won't have any classes together this year."

"Yeah." I realize I don't have a bra on under my ripped and tattered Foo Fighters T-shirt. Maybe he won't notice. "Probably not." It's good we won't have any classes together, though. He's the reason I got a B in the lab. I couldn't focus on anything but him. We had some serious chemistry. Yes, I'm a giant cheese ball for even thinking that, but it's true.

He plunges his hands into his pockets and glances behind him. "Are you going down?"

My mind takes a strange turn while I process his question. All sorts of perverted thoughts run through my head. I would love to go down, thank you very much. The heat in my cheeks intensifies. No, that's not what he's asking. If anything, I should be pissed at him, not turned on by his unintentional dirty talk. He stood me up, after all.

"Um," I say. "Yes, I am going down."

He scoots to the side and holds the door for me, a hint of a smile on his lips. I wonder if he saw everything I've just been thinking written all over my face. God, I hope not.

I step through the doorway with an exaggerated swing of my hips. Always a good reminder for what he could've had.

"Uh, Alexis?"

My name on his tongue sounds amazing, but I try not to notice. I turn, the bulk of my laundry bag holding the door open for me. "What?"

He swallows and glances at his black boots. "It's great to see you again."

I nod. It's great to see him, too, but I'm not the one who didn't show up for our date at the end of last semester and who vanished for an entire summer with no explanation. Maybe he forgot about our non-date, because he sure isn't trying to explain himself. But why didn't he call to tell me he wouldn't be coming instead of making me wait for him?

My bag bites its weight into my shoulder. When I shift it to the other one, the door creaks closed in Ian's face. I wince. I didn't mean for that to happen.

"Well." He frowns through the broken squares in the window. "See you."

"Yeah." With a sigh, I watch him walk away. I've missed our group study sessions where we'd always sit next to each other and accidentally nudge each other's knee or foot. I've missed how easy it is to be with him. I've missed *him*. He doesn't seem like the type who wouldn't call to say he couldn't make it. But he didn't.

I shake my head hard to keep the pity party tears from coming, and face the basement. A single lightbulb dangles from a string at the bottom of the stairs and sways gently back and forth. Shadows hover at the edges of the glow and deepen into black ink in the far corners. My breath hitches in my throat just looking down there, but I'm not sure why, exactly. Basements have never bothered me before. Even the cellar back home doesn't freak me out. But this one feels…I don't know. Off, somehow.

The wooden railing is coated in a thick layer of dust. I move my hand down it and take a step. The boards under my feet groan. A spiderweb tugs at my fingers. I shake it off and take another step.

The air smells dank and stale, like not many people have had the pleasure of breathing down here. A steady hum sounds from the left—probably Ian's clothes in the dryer.

Behind the lightbulb, there's a wall of storage cupboards. Each one is about three feet wide and three feet tall with padlocks hooked into the latches. They're the perfect size for the local serial killer to store his latest victims.

Stop it. We don't even have a serial killer in Lawrence. No one's been murdered since last Christmas when that guy knifed another guy, and that happened clear across town.

I make it to the bottom of the stairs and dash toward the washers and dryers. Everything goes into one washer. I don't bother to separate lights from darks because I don't care that much. A swirl of soap goes on top, and once the lid is closed and quarters are inserted, rushing water drowns out the quiet hum of the running dryer.

Movement to the right catches my eye. One of the storage cupboards slowly swings open. It takes a second for what I'm seeing to sink in. I shrink back. My heartbeat jumps.

The open cupboard door bounces against the one next to it before it stops. I will myself to breathe. These things happen in drafty old basements. Maybe the padlock hadn't been secured. Or maybe someone is in there. I dig my fingernails into my palms to still the nervous quiver in my stomach. I have to get out of here, but my feet are frozen to the concrete floor. I twist my fingers around the bottle of soap and dart my gaze from the cupboard to the stairs. I'm a fast runner, sixth in the state my senior year of high school. My track scholarship helped finance KU. If my feet will move, I can make it out.

Swallowing hard, I manage to take a step. My scalp prickles. I watch the cupboard so hard my eyes burn. Another step. The hairs lift along my arms. It feels as though someone is watching, waiting to leap out. I sprint for the stairs. Terror wells in my throat. I take the steps three at a time and erupt through the door.

Arms. They reach for me.

"Alexis." Ian's face is close to mine, eyebrows pinched together. "What's wrong? What happened?"

I'm shaking under his grasp on my shoulders. My breaths come quick and loud. "The cupboard," I whisper. "In the basement."

"Stay here." He disappears through the door.

Blood roars through my head. My fingers worry at the soap lid, unscrewing and screwing, as if they have a will of their own.

The door creaks open, and Ian comes out. "I didn't see anything but an open cupboard."

"So it was open? I didn't imagine it? Was anything inside?" The words tumble out before I can make sense of them.

"Just boxes." He rubs his hands on his pants, eyes never leaving mine, and steps toward me. "What did you see?"

"The cupboard. It opened by itself." The words sound crazy, even to my ears. I reach for him, a plea to believe me. "I swear it opened by itself."

"Okay." He folds his hand over mine and squeezes gently. "I believe you. Maybe it wasn't latched all the way."

"Maybe." I nod. "I'm sorry, Ian. I'm not usually so irrational."

"I know. You got spooked." His thumb slides across my knuckles, sending a thrill through my body. "No need to say you're sorry."

I look at the door and sigh. "I still have to go down there later to put my clothes in the dryer, though."

"Well, I could do it." He shrugs. "If you want. I have to get mine anyway."

"Can you handle the sight of all my lacy underwear?" Oh my God. I can't believe I just asked that. Fright must do weird things to my mouth filter.

He grins. "I think I can handle it."

I look away. The thought of him putting his hands on my underwear melts warmth through my stomach. Especially the underwear I'm wearing now. I glance at the laundry room door to sweep the thought from my head. "I appreciate the offer, but…maybe…could we just walk down there together?"

"Sure. Can we hang out at your place while we wait, though? My apartment's pretty empty."

I tap my thumb on the soap handle, frowning. It seems risky to let him in and set myself up for another rejection. The last thing I want to do is get hurt again, but I allow myself a single nod. Besides, I don't want to be alone right now, and Tri won't be interested in listening about open cupboards if he thinks it's time to play. "You can meet Tri."

"Tri?" He tilts his head, eyebrows drawn together. "Is that a roommate?"

"He's a cat," I say. "I got him at the end of the school year." After our non-date and my best-friend-slash-roommate moved away because she'd been dumped one too many times, I threw a pity party for myself because it seemed I wasn't worth anyone's time or effort. It's the same feeling that's hung around my shoulders since childhood when Mom left. When Ian didn't show and Elizabeth moved out, I decided I'd had enough abandonment in my life. My pity party involved a slow evolution into a crazy cat lady with the adoption of Tri. "Do you like cats?"

"Uh." He scratches his cheek. "Depends on the cat."

"He's part dog, so…"

Ian laughs. "I'm sure we'll get along fine, then."

I look at our hands twined together. His skin feels rough, especially the tips of his fingers. He must still play guitar. I never got a chance to hear him play, and this shoots an ache into my chest. "You don't have to wait with me."

He closes the space between us and tucks his free hand under my chin. "I want to." A pained expression passes over his face, and then he smiles.

His nearness snags at the air in my lungs. My mouth opens, but I can only nod. We head up the stairs. He doesn't try to take his hand from mine, and neither do I. Maybe that means he feels a tingling stir in his stomach, too. I hope he does.

Gray clouds have washed over the setting sun. The wind has picked up, tossing the ends of my stick-straight hair into my face. I sweep it out of the way and notice that Ian's sharp blue eyes are watching. A smile twitches his lips, and he turns away. I do, too, and wonder at what he might be thinking, what he thinks of me, why he didn't show at the club my favorite band, One Blue Chuck, was to perform.

Sometimes I'd catch him looking at me in lab, even in the middle of our experiments. He'd caught me doing the same thing, too. Our graduate teaching assistant banned us both from the sulfuric acid because neither of us could pay attention.

I root through my pocket for my keys as we near number twenty-six. "So, what were you doing outside the laundry room when I came bursting out? Did you forget something?"

"Uh…" He slips his hand from mine. "I was going to…" He clears his throat and rubs the back of his head. "I was going to ask you on another date and promise to show up this time."

I push my lips together and zip the key in the lock. Is this the part where he apologizes and gives some sort of lame excuse? Because I'm not sure I'm ready to go there.

"Oh" is all I say, and he follows me inside.

He looks around. "It's just like mine."

It's sparse in here since I'm a practical girl, but cozy. A couch sits in front of the television. Original impressionist artwork painted by the guy downtown hangs above the couch. A single plant soaks up the remaining daylight from the balcony window. The smell of my chicken Alfredo dinner lingers in the air.

"It's nice," Ian says.

"Thanks. Hey, Tri," I call. "Come meet Ian."

"What's with his name?" Ian asks.

"Well." I kick off my sandals and look around for the cat. He's usually springing toward me as soon as I walk in the door. "I got him at the humane society, and one of my friends who works there has a four-year-old daughter who named him Triable. She was trying to say triangle because he has triangles all over his head. My friend shortened it to Tri, and now that's the only name he answers to." I slap my legs and make kissy noises. "Come *here*, Tri."

"Ah, I see. So he's a dog dressed in a cat's triangles." Ian slides me a grin. "I like dogs."

I snort out a laugh, but it fades fast. Still no Tri. Then I hear it—a low growl. I follow the sound. It grows louder the closer I get to the kitchen. I gasp when I see the cat, and my hand flutters to my mouth.

He's crouched in front of a lower cupboard door near the far wall. The cupboard door is open. My chest tightens.

Tri's ears are folded back. The hair along his back spikes up. A growl that ends in a hiss spits from his mouth. I've never heard him do that before. The sound makes me shudder.

I turn to Ian, who stood right behind me, and point to the cupboard. "It wasn't open when I left."

He brushes past and steps slowly toward Tri. The cupboard door blocks whatever might be inside. I know I didn't leave this one open, and Tri has no reason to open it, though I don't doubt he could if he wanted to. I follow Ian.

He stops a good distance from Tri and bends over to peer inside the cupboard. "It's just appliances."

Tri peels back his lips to bare needlelike teeth and hisses. It's obviously not just appliances in there.

I march past them both and look inside. Ian's right. Nothing else is in there. I slam the cupboard closed. "What is happening? What's with these cupboard doors opening? Tri…" I reach down to soothe him, but he scuttles off. "Why are you freaking out?" Frustrated tears prick my eyes.

"Hey, calm down." Ian wraps a thick arm around my shoulder and pulls me close. "Maybe Tri opened the cupboard. Maybe he saw his reflection in the toaster or something." His fingers rub strength into my back.

"Maybe." I don't believe it, though. Something opened both cupboard doors, the same something that frightened Tri. I know it. I just don't know what it could be.

Ian presses a kiss to the top of my head. It's such a sweet gesture, it distracts me from the swirl of thoughts in my head. His body is nothing but lean muscle and molds to mine almost perfectly. I inhale his scent, a musky cologne that pumps my blood faster.

Ian is in my apartment. It doesn't seem possible, though I've dreamed about it more times than I care to admit. We did much more than a one-armed hug in my dreams. My skin grows hot. The air shifts and charges, exploding fire in every part of us that touches.

He must sense it, too, because he pulls back, his hand at my elbow, and looks down at me with his lips parted. He brushes a strand of hair from my eyes, blazing a trail of heat with his fingertips. "Alexis?"

His breath sighs over my mouth. My lips tingle. The rest of me aches. "Huh?"

"I want to—"

Something crashes from the back of the apartment, a familiar sound that means Tri probably bumped something off the headboard.

I pull away, my head swimming with the sudden absence of Ian's touch. "It's Tri. I have to find him."

Tri's eyes glow in the near dark under my bed, a mix of yellow and green and pissed off. No amount of kissy noises will coax him from hiding. He's seriously freaked out, poor guy. I can't blame him.

Ian stands in the doorway as I push myself up on the bed. One more step, and he'd be inside my room. A flush creeps up my cheeks. My head and body seem to be reacting to Ian in two totally different ways.

"Is he okay?" he asks. Worry creases his forehead.

I right the vase on top of the headboard. "I think he'll live."

"That's good." He glances around my room, at the overflowing bookcases and the pictures of family and friends on top of the dresser. When his gaze lands on the bed, he bites his lip. It makes me wonder what just went through his head. "I'm sorry about not showing up that night. I'd like to explain everything to you if you'll give me a chance." A grimace washes over his face, but he tries to hide it with a quirk of his mouth.

I have a feeling whatever he wants to tell me has hurt him. Maybe this isn't a simple case of I-had-better-things-to-do-with-my-time. Maybe we were both hurt that night. It surprises me how much I don't like the thought of him in any kind of pain. I step toward him and touch his shoulder. "Okay. But only if you have a beer with me." I could use something to calm my nerves.

He nods. "I could probably be talked into that."

I push him out the door in front of me, using that as an excuse to feel the ripple of muscle under his shirt. He doesn't seem to mind my hand on his back, but I pull my fingers away before either of us can get used to the connection.

In the kitchen, I keep an eye on the cupboard as I near the refrigerator. How many times have I opened it and Tri had no problem with it at all? What changed? Nothing inside the cupboard. I don't have any new appliances that are particularly frightening.

I grab two beers and hand one to Ian. They're Elizabeth's, but she left them behind at our old apartment when she moved out. Ian opens it with his fingers. I'm about to reach for an opener because I'm not as cool as him, when he takes my bottle and opens it for me.

"Thanks," I say. "Let's sit." I gesture to the table against the wall. It's close to the cupboard, which fills me with unease, but I want to see if it opens again.

We sit across from each other. Ian busies himself with spinning the bottle cap, but his eyebrows are bunched together as if he's trying to find the right words. I stroke off the condensation beading from the bottle while I wait for him to start.

Tri slinks across the living room carpet so low his belly touches the floor. He lies like a sphinx, front half on the kitchen linoleum, back half on the carpet—his usual spot while I'm cooking. He thrusts his head out, sniffing the air as though he doesn't trust it. I wish I knew what spooked him.

"That night was going to be amazing," Ian says and sits back in his chair. The bottle cap dances under his expert fingers. "I was going to see One Blue Chuck with my lab partner, who happened to be the most beautiful girl I'd ever seen."

"Wow." A nervous chuckle trips out of my mouth, and I take a long swig. "Thank you."

"You're welcome," he says with a faint smile. He leans forward and cups his hands around his beer. "I got a call from my mom that night. She was crying, and I could barely understand her." He rubs his hand up and down the top of his buzz cut. "After I calmed her down some, she told me my sister was dead."

My mouth pops open. "Oh my God. I'm so sorry." He *was* in pain that night. He's still in pain from the looks of him, and my selfishness and narcissism made me think his no-show all had to do with me. I shake my head at my own stupidity.

"We were close, you know? Me and my sister." A sad smile drifts over his mouth. "We used to watch *The Princess Bride* every weekend before I left for college. We had the entire thing memorized, forward and backward."

I nod. I want to reach out and take his hurt away, but I don't want to interrupt him.

"She fell in with a bad group of friends, and drugs just wasted her away. She didn't have her shit together like I do." He gulps down half his beer with a few bounces of his Adam's apple. "When I hung up with my mom, I threw my phone across the room and it shattered into pieces." He fixes me with his blue eyes and pins me to the spot with how sad they are. "That's why I couldn't call you."

His words have tangled a knot in my throat. I try to swallow past it. "It's okay."

"I should've come by the club to explain everything to you." He shakes his head. "I wasn't thinking straight, though, and my mom…wasn't handling it well. So I went home to her."

I reach my hand across the table. "I'm really sorry."

He takes my hand and squeezes it. "I spent the summer with my mom just to make sure she was okay. I just got here last night and was planning to stalk you at the bookstore tonight. Which would explain the need for clean clothes."

"No need for stalking." I smile. "I'm right here."

"You're right here." His gaze searches my face for a long moment, kicking my heart into double time. His thumb caresses mine. He runs his teeth over his bottom lip.

A powerful urge to kiss him swells through me. The idea pools heat in my stomach. I shift in my chair as I imagine his lips molding with mine, his hands sliding up my shirt, over my breasts. "Maybe we should check our laundry," I say before my mind takes it any further.

"Good idea." He pulls me to my feet, eyes locked on mine.

We step closer to each other, as if laundry is the last thing we're thinking about. The room spins with my need, and I touch my hand to his chest to anchor myself to something solid. His fingers graze my elbow and skim up my arm, my neck, my cheek. Every nerve in my body comes alive.

Thunder booms. Rain starts a steady beat on the roof. The lights dim, then blink back to life.

I pull away, suddenly grateful for the interruption. We can't do this, or rather *I* can't do this. I've already set myself up to be a crazy cat lady. I'm through taking risks with people who will only leave me heartbroken and alone. "We should go before the power goes out."

Ian glances up at the ceiling with a sigh. "Right."

We step past Tri, who hasn't moved from his half-in-the-kitchen, half-out sphinx perch. Worry gnaws at my feet, and I stop. I'm not sure I want to leave him alone if something really is in the cupboard.

"Hey," Ian says. "There's nothing in the cupboard, remember? He'll be fine."

I nod. Of course he'll be fine. He's a cat. Cat-slash-dog. But animal instincts are better than ours, and his are obviously telling him something's wrong. "Tri?" He barely twitches an ear at the sound of his name. I purse my lips. "We'll be right back, buddy."

Outside, wind whips through the trees and flings dirt in mad whirls. Stinging raindrops zip through the rumbling clouds and pelt my skin. We dash down the stairs to the laundry room door.

Raindrops bleed over the red sign. The painted snake scales on the ground float in a small puddle, pushing into one another to form one long line against the edges.

Ian opens the door, and I follow him through. The

lightbulb stutters and buzzes. If it gives out, so will my heart.

"Alexis?" Ian stops. "The cupboard is open."

I curl my fingers into his arm and peer around him. The black mouth of the cupboard yawns open. "Did you close it?"

"Yes."

A cold dread needles up my spine. "Maybe someone else opened it. Or the wind. It has to be a broken latch, like you said." None of these possibilities make me feel any better.

"I'll close it again." Ian starts down the stairs.

I follow, my gaze aimed straight ahead at the cupboard. Boxes are piled inside, some marked CHRISTMAS and BOOKS in black marker. Ian reaches for the cupboard door. A deep chill threads through the cracks between the boxes and sweeps goose bumps over my arms. My next breath catches in the air, then slips away into the darkness.

"It's so cold." My voice trembles. I wrap my arms around myself.

Ian closes the door, and the latch clicks. He secures the padlock and gives it a good tug before turning to me. His eyes widen. "Are your lips turning blue?"

"P-Probably." My whole body quakes so much, it's hard to get the word out.

He folds me into a warm hug and rubs feeling back into my body. "Come on. Let's hurry, and then I'll get you under a blanket."

I nod while his promise brings a welcome flush to my skin. He puts a hand at the small of my back and guides me to the washers and dryers. The heat radiating from his strong fingers helps quiet my chattering teeth.

The washer is finished, but Ian's dryer still hums. He helps me transfer my clothes to the other dryer.

I scoop up the last handful and drop it in the dryer along with the stashed dryer sheet in my pocket. "You got to touch my underwear after all."

"Not all of it." He runs a finger across his lower lip and smiles at the floor.

I dig for the quarters in my other pocket and throw him a wicked grin. "How would you know if I'm wearing underwear or not?"

His gaze wanders down my body and up again, lingering on my chest. I squirm in all the right places while he takes me in. "Underwear. No bra," he says.

I gasp and look down my front. My face ignites into a blush. "You can tell?"

"I can—" His gaze ticks to the left. The naughty glint behind his eyes fades.

I spin around. The cupboard door swings open and knocks against the one next to it. The hair at the back of my neck spikes alert.

"Start your dryer," Ian whispers, "and let's get out of here."

He must feel it, too, the dread that crawls from the cupboard and speeds through my heart. With shaky fingers, I push my quarters into the slot and start the machine. Something rattles inside like loose rocks. I slip my hand into Ian's, and we step toward the stairs.

The lightbulb swings harder in a gust of freezing wind that comes from the cupboard. Another step closer, and the light blinks out. Darkness chokes off my next breath. I crush Ian's hand. A scream climbs up my throat. The light flickers back on.

I scream anyway. A pale gray hand grasps the lower ledge of the open cupboard. It's reaching through the side of one of the boxes. Not out of the box. *Through*. Like the boxes aren't even real. Blackened fingernails claw at the wood, dragging the rest of whatever it is forward. A fountain of dirty blond hair spills out of the box next, followed by another hand. Terror nails me to the floor. I can't look away.

Ian tugs on my arm. "Let's *go*."

Just as we reach the first step, the light snaps off again. I cry out. Glass shatters and rains onto the concrete floor.

Ian trips up the stairs. That thing, it's behind me. A rush of icy air glides fingers over my back. Something snatches my foot, and I fall. My knee smashes into the stairs. An iron grip clasps my other ankle and yanks me to the bottom of the steps.

"Ian!" But he's already there, pulling on my arms. I kick out with my free leg and connect with something solid. The grip around my leg loosens, enough for Ian to heave me to my feet and push me in front of him. We're almost to the top. Lightning flashes and reflects its brilliance in one of the remaining glass squares in the door. I see my face, then Ian's, in the reflection. But nothing over his shoulder.

I rip open the door. As soon as Ian throws himself out, I slam it closed again, then take his hand and race for my apartment.

It's pouring. Wind bends the rain into a diagonal sheet. Ian shouts something, but the storm drives his words back into his mouth. Rain stabs cold needles into my skin. I'm drenched before we reach the stairs.

The storm has thrust the evening into night, and even in the glow of nearby apartment lights, it's hard to see anything. I glance over my shoulder anyway to see if that thing is chasing us, but the rain blinds me. I race forward by touch alone. The slick banister, the vibrations of the metal staircase, and Ian's hand in mine all convince me I'm headed in the right direction. When I think I see number twenty-six on a door, I blink the rain from my eyes and unlock it.

A terrible yowling and hissing comes from inside. The sound sends a violent shudder through my bones. "Tri!" I sprint into the kitchen, Ian at my heels.

A girl. A girl with filthy blond hair. She's leaning out of the open cupboard. Her hands are wrapped around Tri, who's clawing and fighting and biting. She jerks him to her chest and turns her head toward us. One milky blue eye peers through the dirty curtain of her hair while she drags herself and Tri into the cupboard. The door slams shut behind her.

Tri's gone. The silence and his absence kick into my stomach, doubling me over. But instead of buckling to the ground, I'm running forward. I tear open the cupboard. Behind all the appliances is a large hole, and behind that is a tangle of pipes over a brick wall.

"Tri!"

A faint meow answers my call from deep inside the hole. I heave a choked cry and fling a toaster and blender out by their cords.

Ian's by my side, tossing everything out, then he climbs into the cupboard and peers into the hole. "Do you have a flashlight?"

I nod and search the hall closet for one that works. What just happened? Did a girl really just crawl through the cupboard and take my cat? A sob shakes through my shoulders. Tears slide down my face, mixing with the rain that streams down my body and puddles at my feet. I hand Ian the flashlight, and he shines the beam down into the hole.

"I can't see a thing," he says. "It's too dark down there."

"We have to go to the laundry room. The cupboards," I say between sobs, "they must be connected somehow. That girl…"

Ian climbs out, face pale, eyes wide, and folds me into his arms. "Who was she? Have you seen her before?"

I crumble against him, but there's no time to mourn the loss of my best, most loyal friend. I pull away. Tri would never willingly abandon me, and I would never abandon him. "I don't know who or what she is, but she can't have Tri."

"I think I know what she is, but we have to be sure."

"What is she?"

He pulls a phone from his back pocket and taps his fingers

across the keys. "A ghost."

"What?" The logical part of me screams *there's no such thing as ghosts*, but the broken, Tri-less part demands I listen. Besides, what else could climb through boxes and disappear through cupboards? "What would a ghost want with a cat?"

"Life force." He shakes his head at his phone. "The more they feed on, the stronger they'll get."

Life force. Does that mean the girl is going to kill Tri? No. No, no, no. I can't think that. Tri is the only thing I can depend on to be there for me. A cat taught me to trust again after Mom, Ian, and Elizabeth left. Sad, but true. Ghost or no ghost, I have to get him back. I fist my hands and glare at the cupboard. "I'm going down there."

Ian grabs my wrist. "Alexis, wait. We have to be sure the girl's a ghost." He shows his phone to me. "That's her, right?"

A picture of a blond girl fills the screen, maybe just a few years younger than me. Her eyes are a dark blue and filled with sadness despite her half smile. The caption underneath reads "Reagan Chain, age 18." "I think so," I say.

"The newspaper archives show that she was murdered in 2009. Her body was hidden inside the basement of…" Ian's gaze tracks over the screen again and again. "Inside the basement of Heartland Apartments."

My stomach rolls. I press a hand to my mouth. The kitchen walls press in. The cupboard in the laundry room is where she was hidden. It makes sense. I knew it when I first saw those cupboards. They're perfect for stashing bodies in. I choke on a gag.

"Richard Donovan, later accused of Reagan's murder, was found dead inside…" Ian stares at me, eyes wide. "His kitchen cupboard."

Everything clicks into place. I shrink away from the open cupboard in my kitchen. The murderer Richard's old kitchen.

"Apartment twenty-six," we say together.

"It must've started out as a vengeance thing with Reagan, then it morphed into gaining more power from people's life forces because…" Ian glances at me, his forehead wrinkled.

"Because what?" I ask, not at all sure I want the answer.

He winces. "Because in June 2011, another girl was found dead—"

"Inside her kitchen cupboard," I finish for him and swallow. Of all the apartments to rent in Lawrence, I had to choose one haunted by a serial killer ghost. And one that a corporeal killer had lived in. Just my luck. No wonder the girl at work gave me an odd look when I told her I moved here in July. No wonder the rent was so cheap. But this is where the haunting ends. Right here, right now.

"Friends said this girl was doing laundry, and then she stopped texting them." Ian blinks up from the screen, the light casting a strange glow over his face. "It must start in the laundry room then, and when someone from apartment twenty-six goes down there…"

"I'm never doing laundry here again," I say through gritted teeth.

Ian stashes his phone in his back pocket. "At least now we know Reagan's not a demon."

"*What?*"

"After my sister died, my mom thought she was a ghost. She wasn't, but I did a lot of research on ghosts and demons to make sure. It was my mom's grief. Guilt, maybe. She was haunted by all of it. Not my sister." He frowns. "My mom wasn't ready to let go."

I bite the inside of my cheek at the pain in his voice. It makes me wonder when he found time to grieve for his sister if he was chasing away his mom's imaginary ghosts the whole summer. "And if Reagan was a demon?"

Ian's blue eyes bore into mine. "Then neither of us would be going back down there." He takes the saltshaker from the table and pockets it. "Salt can't get rid of demons, but it's supposed to send ghosts to the other side. It's pure. It's from the earth, just as ghosts' human forms once were. But ghosts aren't from the earth. They can't handle salt's purity."

"It's *supposed* to send them to the other side." This is crazy. All of it. How can this even work? But I don't have a better idea, so this has to work for Tri's sake. A well-loved toy mouse sits on the end of the counter next to the microwave, exactly where Tri left it. I press my lips together. "Ready?"

He turns the flashlight off and on, then swallows. "Ready."

We dart back out into the storm. The wind jackknifes into me as I quickly lock the door. It presses me sideways, urging me toward the laundry room and Tri. My hand tucked in Ian's, we run. The rain follows the wind and stings my head and back. We slip down the stairs, the metal crisscrosses too soaked to provide any traction.

I open the laundry room door, and Ian enters first. The flashlight beam jabs through the darkness onto the open cupboard below. We slowly descend the stairs while he shines the light in the deepest corners of the basement. My stomach clenches with each step, with each shadow the beam shines through. There's no sign of Tri or the girl.

"Tri?" I whisper. Silence except for the low hum and rattle of the dryers.

We reach the bottom of the stairs, and I step toward the open cupboard. Our shoes crunch over the glass from the broken lightbulb. Broken shards catch the flashlight beam in winks.

Ian hands the light to me and steps toward the dryers. A chill breezes over my fingertips as I reach for one of the top boxes inside the cupboard. It's heavier than I expect, so I set the flashlight on the bottom ledge, right where the girl's hand was when she started to climb out through the boxes. Shivers flash across my back at the memory. I tug at the box with both hands and drop it to the ground. Behind that box is another box. How deep does this cupboard go?

"Tri? Are you in there?" Nothing. A strangled sob pushes through the knot in my throat.

Ian roots through the clothes in his dryer, then holds a sweatshirt out to me. "You'll catch cold down here in your wet clothes. Put this on."

I take it since I think I'll be able to unload the cupboard faster if I can stop shaking. The fabric is almost hot and it brings feeling back into my fingers so I can move them again. I hurry into the sweatshirt.

Ian shrugs into one, too, and then helps me fling out boxes. Clouds of dust roll up and cling to the tears and rain on my face. The back wall appears. Just a few more boxes left.

The tip of my nose is numb and my fingertips ache with cold. Ian slides the last box out of the cupboard. Something cracks inside when it lands on the concrete. I grab the flashlight, sit on the ledge, and swing myself inside the cupboard feet first.

Ian climbs in with me. I have to smash myself against the side to allow him room. The flashlight carves deep shadows all over his face, but I can tell he's looking at me in the confined space.

Without a word, we both kick at the far wall. I slam my feet against it with everything I have. We soon punch through into nothingness.

Arctic air gusts over my body. I gasp as the chill seeps over my skin and stitches ice into my lungs.

"Ah, that's cold." Ian adjusts his position and aims the flashlight through the hole.

I climb out of the cupboard and back in again headfirst so I can see out, too. Dust hovers in the air so thick I can taste it. A foot ahead is a brick wall covered in a maze of pipes, one of which leaks a steady dribble. The wall stretches several yards right and left, but the light can't penetrate the darkness above.

It's a black hole up there, eating everything that touches it.

"What is this place?" I ask.

Each shaky breath through Ian's blue lips clouds the air. "Some kind of tunnel m-maybe?"

I poke my head through the hole. "T-Tri?" My teeth chatter so loud, the sound bounces off the brick wall. A meow from above answers me. That single sound rushes relief to my heart. He's still alive. Tears spring into my eyes as I back my head through the hole. "Did you hear that?" I ask, just to be sure I didn't imagine it.

"I heard him. We've got to get him away from her." He wraps an arm around me, his whole body trembling. His other hand fishes for the salt in his pocket.

I tuck myself under his chin and shiver uncontrollably. "Why is it so cold?"

"It's her," he breathes into my hair. He tilts the saltshaker so it pours into his trembling hand. Some sifts through his fingers and lands just inside the hole. He makes a fist over the grains left in his palm. "Now we wait for her to come."

I lean out of the hole and shine the beam upward into the tunnel. Complete darkness hovers above. The pipe drips. My heart pounds. I look at Ian. "Give me some—" Winter brushes against my fingers on the edges of the hole. I jerk back and scoot away.

Ian's jaw pulses. He clenches his fist and inches closer to the hole.

The girl appears instantly in front of the brick wall. She flashes an arm out and snatches Ian by the neck. She rips him from the cupboard, and he vanishes out of the hole without a sound. One of his boots teeters on the jagged edges of the broken wall, then falls over in front of the pipes with a heavy *thud*.

"Ian!" I shine the light upward into the black hole. "Tri!" Silence. Nothing answers. Not even a meow. "No." A deep, bone-quaking shudder rolls through me. The beam skips over the brick wall and bounces all over the empty cupboard when I lean back inside.

They're gone. They're both gone. I'm all alone. I squeeze my eyes shut and then open them again, but the cupboard is still empty. It really happened. My breaths come too fast, too loud. I think I might pass out.

I collapse against the wall of the cupboard and shine the light on the ceiling with both hands. The bright spot helps me focus. Salt. I need more salt. I touch the dusting of it below the hole and pinch a few grains between my fingers.

A burst of chilly wind rushes through the hole. Icy fingers grip my neck. They drag me forward to the hole, face to face with the ghost. Her milky blue eyes are cold and murderous. The flashlight drops from my hand and rocks its beam in wild arcs around the cupboard. She squeezes, crushing the air from my lungs. I claw at her hand, try to peel it off. Salt grains wedged under my fingernails rub over her stone cold skin.

Her grip falters, but I still can't breathe. Her gaze drops to her hand around my throat. Black veins sizzle over her skin, up her arm, and to her neck. It sounds like she's baking.

"Alexis!" Ian calls from above.

White spots burst behind my eyes. I want to answer, but I can't. My lungs blaze with need.

Tiny snowflakes fall on the girl's head. They burn into her face until one of her eyes sags halfway down her cheek. She shoves me back into the cupboard and vanishes.

I drag in one breath before I topple out of the cupboard and crack my head on the concrete floor.

I don't know how long I'm out. Seconds, minutes, hours, it's all too long. Ian and Tri need me. I could never abandon them. I prop myself up on one arm. The basement sways and pitches my stomach's contents dangerously close to my mouth. I take several deep breaths and touch the back of my head. There's a massive bump back there, and my fingers come away bloody. But I'm alive. My throat feels cracked and raw, but I'm breathing.

Posting my arms underneath me, I stumble to my feet. The flashlight is behind one of the boxes littering the floor. Its glow is as bright as ever, so I must not have been out too long. I take one step at a time up the stairs since each one drives a spike through my head.

Outside, the sharp wind and pelting rain help clear the cobwebs from my brain. I need salt. A lot of it. When I have it in my hand, I'm going to ram it down ghost bitch's throat.

I drag myself up the second set of stairs to my apartment, hissing through my teeth at the pain gnawing at my head. Lightning forks across the sky and illuminates just how dark it is. All the lights in the apartment building have gone out.

Thunder booms a warning when I reach number twenty-six. I plug my key into the lock. It's quiet inside except for the drops of rain falling from me to the carpet and my heart jumping inside my chest. I flick the light switch just in case the power outage will somehow not affect me. Nothing happens. I sweep the flashlight beam over every dark corner, and then I take a step forward.

Something creaks, long and loud from the kitchen. My breaths scrape along my raw throat and fog the chilled air. Reagan's here, waiting. I can feel it.

I bare my teeth like some crazed animal and turn the corner. She's slinking out of the cupboard on all fours. She stops when she sees me with the melted eye that's now almost to her chin.

The big container of salt is in the cupboard to the left of the sink. I set the flashlight on the counter so the beam casts over her. Her freaky eye squints into the light, and she crouches low behind the cupboard door, ready to spring.

I scratch my nails against my palms and swallow. The salt is on the second shelf, buried behind other spices because the container is so big. I can see its exact location in my head. Thunder rumbles through the walls and floor and charges urgency through my gut. I lick my lips, and then I rush forward.

The ghost jumps from her crouch at the same time. She's fast. I'm faster. Maybe the salt has already weakened her. I open the cupboard and knock everything over in my hurry. My fingers grasp the salt just as hers slide around my neck. Her glacial touch needles my skin. She clamps my windpipe shut and drags me toward the cupboard. I fumble to get the container open. It slips from my fingers, but I shift my body at the last second to wedge it between me and the counter.

She locks her other hand around my throat, still pulling me forward. Alarm bells sound in my head. My chest burns. The edges of my vision start to dim. My throat makes a ticking sound as though it's marking my final seconds.

The salt opens. I jerk the container toward her face so a stream hits her other eye. It drips down the side, but it's not quite even with the other. She releases me and I crumble to the floor, dragging in air. The black veins webbing her gray skin branch off again and again until they cover her entire body. They even trace under the thin fabric of her dingy dress. She takes a step back toward the cupboard.

Between gulps for more air, I fling salt at her. It sprays her whole body. A rotten, sulfur smell punches into my stomach. I swallow a gag and crawl forward to shoot more salt at her. Black veins crack through her melted eyes. She throws her head back in a silent scream, then vanishes.

I crush the salt to my chest and lean against a lower cupboard. My heart knocks against my ribs, beating on the wood behind me.

A low moan sounds from the open cupboard, deep and familiar.

"Ian?" I crawl forward. Grains of salt stick to my palms. It's all over the tiles.

Ian climbs out of the cupboard and collapses on the floor. The hole in the wall seals itself up as he pulls his feet through. Deep cuts mark his face and arms, and his sweatshirt and jeans are covered in rips and holes. Tri perches on his chest and licks his eyelids. I bury my face in Tri's side and inhale his sweet scent. His loud purr rumbles his chest. Relief swells through mine.

I touch the side of Ian's face. "Are you okay?" My voice sounds scratchy, as though I've swallowed claws.

"I think so." He groans. "Why's Tri licking my eyelids?"

I bark out a laugh that ends in a sob. "Because you're both alive."

"He wedged himself behind the pipes so far, I don't think even a ghost could've gotten him. I wiggled my fingers at him and he came right out, though." Ian sets the small saltshaker gripped in his fist down to glide his fingers over Tri's head, and Tri stops his licking to lean into his touch. "This isn't comfortable, kitty."

"Okay." I pluck Tri off him and help ease Ian into a sitting position next to the cupboard. "Better?"

"Better." He runs his hands down his face and winces as his fingers meet the scratches. The open cupboard door blocks some of the glow from the flashlight and paints his face with shadows. "She gone?"

"She's gone. I mean, I guess. I've never done that before." But I do think she's gone. The heavy feeling of dread doesn't press in on me, and Tri isn't hissing anymore. She has to be gone. I collapse next to Ian, careful not to brush too hard against his cuts, and suck in a long breath. Tri tucks his paws underneath him so he looks like a kitty loaf and gazes at

Ian and me. I swear there's a little smile under that Hitler mustache. "Salt. I never would've guessed."

Ian studies his feet, one booted and the other socked. "You don't remember the yellow bubbles in our chemistry books? The ones on the side of the text about chemists' weird quirks and folklore about different elements?"

"Kind of." I never paid attention to those bubbles. I was too busy cramming the things I knew would be on the test into my head.

"There was one in the chapter about sodium. It had to do with sodium chloride and ghosts. Whenever Tri started hissing back there, I'd just fling some out and hope I hit her." He nods at the saltshaker beside him.

I look up at the set of his jaw, at the curl of his dark eyelashes. "Did you get an A in chemistry?"

"Nope. A C-plus. And I blame you for that, by the way."

"Me?" I raise my eyebrows, all innocent-like. "What did I do?"

He holds me closer and rests his forehead on mine. "You're too distracting." His breath tickles my ear.

My body warms. In a crazy way, sitting on the kitchen floor in the near-dark during a thunderstorm with Ian is almost romantic. If it weren't for Reagan getting uncomfortably close to killing us, it *would* be romantic. I lean in closer, my mouth just inches from his. "I could say the same about you."

"You could, huh?" His smile drips into his voice, making it huskier, sexier. He plays with the bottom hem of my sweatshirt, scrunching it between his fingers so his knuckles graze my side. The skin-on-skin contact quickens my breaths. His gaze dips to my mouth, and he skims his tongue over his lower lip. "My clothes look good on you."

"I know." I slide a hand up over his holey sweatshirt and across the curves of his muscles. His heart leaps against my palm. Something builds inside my body, a throbbing for him to touch the deepest part of me. He's making it so easy to forget all my abandonment issues and just go for it. But a lingering doubt still weighs heavily on my heart. Can I handle it if something goes wrong between us? Is it possible to blur the line between crazy cat lady and normal girlfriend?

The lights click back on with a short buzz. Ian grins, and his electric blue eyes brighten. My heart stutters. Jeez, he's pretty.

"There you are." His grin slips into a frown, and his forehead creases. "Is that blood on your neck? Are you bleeding?"

"I cracked my head in the laundry room. But it's nothing."

"Let me see." He pulls away to examine my head.

I try not to wince even though his touch is gentle.

"That's a massive bump you got there. You might have a concussion," he says. "We should get you to the hospital to be sure."

"No." I shake my head. "Just…stay with me. If I'm seeing double in the morning, I'll go to the hospital. I promise."

"Okay. If you say so." His eyebrows are still bunched together, though. He takes my hands in his and pulls me to my feet. "Let's at least get you cleaned up."

I nod and glance at the hills of salt on the linoleum. The overhead glow casts a new light over my kitchen, accentuating the scuffmarks along the floor and the rows of cupboards lining both walls.

There's no way I can stay here. Classes start soon, and I could never leave Tri alone, not after what's happened. Not in a place haunted by ghosts, even with salt in every cupboard. It creeps me out enough to be living in the same place as a killer and where three people, almost five and a cat, died.

Ian cups a palm around my cheek. He searches my eyes so deeply, it feels like he's memorizing my soul, like he knows exactly what I've been thinking. "Stay at my place. *I'll* take the couch and you can have the bed, just until you find a place of your own."

"Really?" I flutter a hand to my throat at the mousy squeak in my voice.

"Yeah. Really."

"Tri, too?"

He wriggles his fingers at Tri, who watches them with big green eyes. "Tri, too."

Whoa. Staying with Ian. That's quite a leap, but he's only trying to be helpful. He's not asking me to move in with him or anything. "Well..." I have to do this for Tri, because where else is he going to stay? Dropping him off somewhere isn't an option. "I'll take the couch."

"Whatever you want." Ian pulls his palm away from my cheek, a smile playing across his mouth.

"Let me just grab a few things first?" But before I do, I open the salt container, my gaze bouncing from cupboard to cupboard, and toss some inside all of them. When I finish, Ian tilts his head at me, a quizzical look on his face. "Just in case," I say, then I hurry down the hallway to throw a few things in a bag.

Once Tri is bundled inside his cat carrier and I've triple-checked to see I have all his and my necessities, the three of us head to Ian's place. A light sprinkle plops on the raincoat draped over Tri's carrier and ripples the many puddles at our feet. The night smells as if it's been washed clean of its horrors. I breathe deep.

Number twelve is on the ground floor. It's bare except for a few boxes, a couch, and his guitar case propped in a corner of the living room. He's right—my apartment is just like his. He sets Tri's litter box in a closet off the kitchen while I set Tri free.

"Come on out, buddy. It's okay," I say. "There aren't any ghosts here."

Tri sniffs the air, then patrols the apartment. It's nothing but business underneath all his triangles and behind that Hitler mustache. I can see it in his serious olive eyes and the rigid stand of his tail. I follow close behind and fling salt into every cupboard I see just in case another ghost decides to crawl out with a wicked life force craving. Salt has just become the number one most sacred item. Never mind quarters.

Once I've salted every cupboard in the kitchen, Ian takes a wet towel and sponges off the blood from my neck with one hand resting on my hip. I take the opposite corner to wash the cuts on his face.

"You're going to have to take your sweatshirt off," I say, doing my best to sound clinical.

He grins. "You first."

I lift an eyebrow. "I thought you liked your clothes on me."

"I changed my mind." His fingers dig ever so slightly into my hip. "They look awful. And how else am I going to clean up all that blood that's run down your neck?"

"Hmm." I bite back a smile. My heartbeat speeds at where this is going. The throbbing ache inside me multiplies. I lift the sweatshirt, along with my T-shirt, slowly over my bare breasts and head, enjoying the slight tremble that rolls over my skin with the fabric.

He slides his gaze over my naked torso. The blazing need in his eyes burns a flush through my skin. He takes his shirt off in a hurry. He's been sculpted from granite, rock-hard but smooth. The cuts on his chest aren't as bad as his face, but I nurse them anyway. While I wash them, his hands explore my torso, grazing my back, skimming the sides of my breasts with his thumbs. Heat floods to my core at his touch. My breaths come in pants and my eyes sink closed.

"You're gorgeous," he murmurs.

I say something unintelligible, but what I really want to do is not talk at all. Screw my emotional baggage. Ian's already proved he's worth the risk, and I can't take this ache anymore. I slip my hand up behind his head, pulling him forward. He doesn't need any more of an invitation. He dips his head down, mouth parted and ready. I'm caught in the hungry pull of his eyes before he sweeps his lips over mine. That alone steals the breath from my lungs.

He kisses me again with a touch more force, and I drink him in deep to savor his sweet taste. I slide my other hand around his head, urging him on. His short hair scrapes over my palms. He flicks his tongue across my lip, and we both sigh into each other's mouths, as though this is where we've always wanted to be.

I close my eyes at the rush of his mouth and the feel of his skin. He drops a trail of kisses down my neck, which draws a moan through my lips. His skin stretches warm and smooth over his muscles and into the dip of his backbone. I gently scratch my nails up the length of it. He groans and brings his lips to mine again.

His kisses are even more urgent. Our breathing becomes erratic. My body is responding in full, and I press against him as hard as I can so he can feel the heat spreading through me.

He pulls away. His eyes are closed, and his chest heaves. "Alexis."

"What?" I breathe. His touch still hums over my skin even though he stands a foot away.

"I've wanted to do that since the first day of lab." He grins.

I peer at him under the fringes of my bangs. "Me, too. And more." My face burns, but it's the truth.

He comes closer and presses a kiss to the corner of my mouth. "Me, too," he says against my lips.

I loop my arms around him again. His kisses paint a glaze over my brain, leaving me more than a little cloudy. It has to be his mouth doing this and not a possible concussion. Head injuries don't leave me breathless and pining for more.

He moves his body so I'm wedged between the counter and him. His growing interest presses against my thigh, and I squirm against his heat. He heaves a low groan that vibrates through his chest into mine. I can't help but smile at the way my body affects him. It makes me feel bold, more so than I ever have. I scoot my butt up on the countertop so I can wrap my legs around his waist and rock my hips against him.

"Oh my God, Alexis." He brings his mouth to my breast, and his circling tongue almost drives me over the edge. I push against him, tuck my fingers into his waistband, and lead him to the bedroom. We're doing this whether he likes it or not, but I'm sure he will. I want him and not just for his body. I want *all* of him.

Trust threads between us as we scatter each other's wet clothes on the way. He's not going anywhere—I feel it in the way he's looking at me, eyes filled with warmth and awe underneath his need. Once a condom is rolled on, he's inside me, coaxing the ache between my legs to explode into relieved bliss. Just like the bottle cap, I dance under Ian's expert touch until his deep thrusts push me into rippling, toe-curling ecstasy. It doesn't take long, and eventually he's there, too, sighing my name into my hair. We collapse back on the pillows, our heavy pants filling the room.

Ian weaves his fingers through mine and brings them to his lips. "Amazing," he breathes.

I curl myself into him and press a kiss to his shoulder. Our bodies fit together so well. We should've been together long ago. "Ian? I'll definitely go out with you, and it's not just the great sex afterglow that's talking, either. Or the fact that you saved Tri."

At the mention of his name, Tri leaps onto the foot of the bed. He sniffs around, then settles himself between our feet for bath time.

"It's also not the fact that I got a higher grade than you in chemistry." This makes Ian laugh, and he pokes me lightly in the ribs. "It's because you're an absolute sweetheart."

He turns on his side and skims the hair from my face. "My mom raised me right." He grimaces, and I can guess at what he's thinking.

"I'm sure your mom raised *both* of you right." I slide my hand over his chest as if I can somehow piece together his broken heart. "Your sister just made bad choices."

"Yeah." He nods and glides his fingertips up and down my arm.

Tri shoots to his feet and stiffens. His gaze is aimed out the open bedroom door. The hair along his back bristles.

One glance at Ian, and we're both untangling ourselves from the blankets and each other. We stand on either side of the bed, both of us completely naked, ticking our eyes from Tri to the doorway. Adrenaline pumps my blood faster until it roars inside my head.

It can't be Reagan again. The salt got rid of her. The three of us wait, unmoving. Seconds pass. My heart drums.

Tri springs off the bed and races down the hall. Ian and I are right behind him. Tri stops at the bathroom and crouches low. He spits a menacing growl and slinks backward.

The cupboard below the sink is open. The one cupboard I forgot to salt.

"We're leaving." I slam the bathroom door and scoop up Tri.

We fly out the door barely dressed with our few necessities and then we're driving away. When we're parked in front of a hotel that I'm pretty sure accepts pets, Ian lifts Tri's cat carrier from the backseat.

"No more Heartland Apartments. Hell, no more apartments *period*," he says, holding my gaze over the trunk of the car. "Deal?"

I readjust the bag over my shoulder to pat my pocket with the salt inside for the hundredth time since we left. "But Reagan...or *somebody* entered a cupboard in *your* apartment, not just number twenty-six. What if it goes after someone else?"

"We could board up the laundry room since that's where it seems to start. We can knock on every door and tell people to stock up on salt if they want to live there. We're never going back inside that laundry room, though. I don't care that our clothes are still down there." He circles the car and holds his hand out to me.

I take it with a smile. "Deal."

"Next time, we can go to the Laundromat. I hear they have a quarter machine."

He catches my laugh with a kiss.

Acknowledgments

The following people deserve copious amounts of hugs and chocolate because of their help and support with this story:

Gabe and Jesse for being my inspiration for Ian and Tri.

Lisa Sills, my fantastic critique partner.

My parents, who nurtured the dark corners of my imagination just as they did the bright, fluffy parts.

The entire Entangled crew for taking a chance on me, but especially my editors, Kaleen Harding and Libby Murphy. You ladies are brilliant. Thank you.

About the Author

Lindsey R. Loucks works as a school librarian in rural Kansas. When she's not discussing books with anyone who will listen, she's dreaming up her own stories. Eventually her brain gives out, and she'll play hide-and-seek with her cat, put herself in a chocolate-induced coma, or watch scary movies alone in the dark to reenergize.

She's been with her significant other for almost two decades.

Check out her website for more information and to contact her. She would love to hear from you! http://www.lindseyrloucks.com